The Ride Of Your Life!

Skeever Dee's Guidance Dream

By Sherry Sayles Varkonyi
Illustrated by Tara Thomas-Sanderson

Published by Destiny's Train Publishing

ISBN 978-1-5233-3498-8

Editing by Kristine M. Smith at wordwhisperer.net

Cover by Margethechicken at fiverr.com

Formatting by bookow.com

Author's Dedication

*To my amazing father, who called losing his arm
"a bump in the road." I have your briefcase.
May I also have your giving and forgiving heart.*

*And to my niece Jamie, the real Ms. Smart,
who has taught me much about
perseverance, priorities and passion.*

Illustrator's Dedication

*To my sweet mommy who has always taught me
to believe and follow my dreams.*

*And to my three beautiful children,
Nathan, Elijah and Nateli,
my inspiration for everything.*

Skeever Dee's early morning swim gave her such joy that she did a few underwater somersaults before entering the lodge.

Shaking off her fur, Skeever kissed Papa Beaver on the cheek. Returning the kiss, he smiled. "Study hard in school today, Skeever, so you can follow in my footsteps when you are older."

Papa took one more gulp of coffee, grabbed his briefcase, and headed out the door. The twins, Sean and Shawna, picked up their lunches and book bags to go to school.

"Papa can see good things for you in the future, dear," Skeever's Mama said.

Skeever sighed loudly. "But I don't want to take over his business, Mama. I want to write amazing stories instead."

"Don't worry about that, Skeever," said Mama wisely. "You just keep writing. Things will work out."

That afternoon as Skeever was leaving her classroom after school, her teacher spoke to her. "Skeever Dee, there is a city-wide writing contest coming soon. Would you like to enter a biography?"

Skeever was instantly excited. "Yes, Ms. Smart! I'd love that!" Right away Skeever began thinking about who would be the subject of her biography.

"What about Helen Keller?" Skeever suggested after sharing her good news of the contest with Mama. "She showed others how to make a difference even though she was blind and deaf."

"Or Abraham Lincoln who was President during the War Between the States?" Mama offered.

As Skeever snuggled into bed, her mind swirled with thoughts of well-known people who had inspired her and many others. When she finally fell asleep, she had a crazy dream.

She found herself in the front car of a ride at an amusement park. The brightly-colored sign at the entrance to the ride read: The Ride of Your Life!

As the car began to climb inside the dark tunnel, Skeever started to feel afraid. Then she heard a mother softly singing a lullaby while rocking a baby boy. It helped Skeever calm down.

The car kept climbing. On Skeever's left, she heard chickens clucking and saw the same boy, about five years old, gathering eggs in a barn.

Climbing still higher, she heard the crack of a baseball bat and cheers from a crowd as she watched the boy, perhaps ten now, hit a home run.

The next morning, Skeever shared her dream with Mama. "That's quite a detailed dream," Mama said.

"But that was only part of it." Skeever spoke softly now. "The car slowed down to a stop and then everything went very quiet. I saw the boy as a teenager. He was in a hospital bed with his left shoulder wrapped in bandages. It looked like his mom and dad leaning over him. This part of the dream made me very sad, Mama."

Mama nodded and asked gently, "Then what happened?"

Skeever's eyes grew wide. "As soon as I understood how hurt he was, the car jerked forward, reached the top of the ride and whizzed down the other side. I hung on as tightly as I could while seeing even more of his experiences."

"Your dream seems very real to you," Mama noticed as Skeever clutched the chair next to her.

Skeever nodded in agreement. "As real as you are to me right now, Mama!"

"I saw him finish college and start his own business. He married a lovely lady, and he played golf, too," Skeever faithfully reported.

Suddenly Skeever knew whose story she would tell! She worked hard to write an amazing biography.

With a hopeful heart, she gave her entry to Ms. Smart.

"Thank you, Skeever Dee. The winners' names will be announced in two weeks," she added.

Two weeks seemed a long time to wait, but finally Ms. Smart spoke to the class. "Students, I have exciting news! Skeever Dee has placed third in the Children's Writing Contest. She will be reading her biography next Monday night in the school gym." Skeever's classmates cheered!

On her big night, the school gymnasium was packed with parents, teachers and students. As Skeever walked to the microphone to read her biography, she could see Mama and Papa sitting in the front row.

In a strong voice, she shared how her subject lost his left arm in an accident on the farm when he was sixteen years old and the changes he had to make in his life.

"When he no longer had two hands to play the trumpet in the band anymore, he switched to harmonica," Skeever said proudly. "The pain in his shoulder never quite stopped, but he refused to take drugs or feel sorry for himself."

"He didn't quit, but worked as hard as ever. He served on the City Council," Skeever told the crowd.

"He even chopped wood, taught his kids to ice skate, and helped them with their homework."

By the time she neared the end of her story, nearly everyone in the room had tears in their eyes. Looking up from the page (for she knew the last line by heart), Skeever exclaimed, "I'm so glad that this gentleman is with us tonight so I can introduce him to you! Papa, would you please come up on the stage!"

Everyone shouted with surprise, then clapped and cheered as Papa joined his daughter at the microphone. Giving Skeever a big hug, he said to her, "You have a real way with words, Skeever Dee. I am very proud of you!"

"Thank you, Papa," Skeever answered. "I am just doing what you've always taught me to do, and that is to follow my dreams!"

Skeever's heart felt so full that she thought it might burst with joy. A photographer came to take their picture as she and Papa grinned as only beavers can.

Discussion Questions

1. What did Skeever see and hear in her dream?

2. What were some of the emotions Skeever experienced during her dream?

3. Who was the dream about?

4. How did the dream help guide Skeever?

5. What did Skeever decide to do after having her dream?

6. What were some of the lessons Skeever and Papa learned from the dream?

7. Did anyone else in the book have a dream?

Take Aways

A guidance dream gives us direction and input that help take us further down the road. Perhaps we are stuck without answers. We may be on the verge of a great breakthrough, or need to see things more clearly. Guidance dreams shed light on our situation and give us clarification and a certainty of the next step, and possibly even the big picture. It brings that "a-ha" moment and we're off and running.

Skeever Dee wants to be a writer, but Papa hopes she will take over his business instead. The opportunity for her to enter a biography contest at a city-wide level is a perfect way to display her writing skills, but it's important to pick the right subject for the work. In a dream, she is shown an unlikely and unknown candidate by watching his life, a little at a time.

Skeever's dream has some interesting symbols:

· She was not driving the car, but was being taken through the ride on water, often representing guidance by another.
· The ups and downs of the ride were like the ups and downs of Papa's life.
· The scenes were very real where she could hear and see all the elements as well as feel many emotions. Some dreams are like that—intense!
· Skeever knew enough about Papa's life to recognize the dream was about him. If Mama put two and two together, she never let on.

We all have our own dream language based on our personal experiences and knowledge. Skeever Dee was shown how amazing Papa's story was and how it needed to be told. That specific biography was the key that helped Papa understand about his daughter's talent like nothing else could have done. In that respect, it also carried some attributes of an identity (or destiny) dream.